P9-CLO-195

Who Would You Be?

Written by Kim Johnson
Illustrated by Jill E. Buffington

Copyright © 2015 Kim Johnson
All rights reserved
BuLu is a trademark of Inspired Girl
Productions

ISBN:1511965975

To my daughter Madison,

I love you more than words can describe. I am
beyond proud of the young woman you have
become. I am humbled by what you have taught me.
Thank you for being so amazing.

We all remember being asked what we wanted to be when we grew up. Most of the time when we answered, there would be an opinion to follow our answer. The very first time I can remember my father asking me, I answered, "teacher". I loved school and the thought of being like my beloved Mrs. Walker thrilled me. My father, however, had much higher aspirations for me, a teacher was not what he wanted for me.

He didn't hide his reservations. Immediately, he explained all the reasons this was not a good idea. I adored my father, so I began to think maybe I was not going to be a teacher.

Fast forward to seventh grade, I was in love with my literature class and my teacher, Mrs. Dean. My love of books and words reaches a new level and I begin to feel the burning desire to be a writer. Once again, I shared my idea with my father. Once again, he let me know that this is not a profession that will make me any money. Once again, I chose to quiet my desire.

Today I am a peak performance coach (really a teacher), a writer, and an artist. After ignoring my internal calling from all of these parts of myself for the early part of my life, I now embrace them wholeheartedly. They are my life.

We all have stories like this, and they all began when we were children. Seemingly innocent questions asked to a child can trigger beliefs that don't serve them long term.

Without any ill intent, these questions and statements, put into play a lifelong belief system that can truly impact a child.

We are extremely careful with our children's belief systems. What empowers them? What allows them to believe in their greatness? What develops their compassion? What do they love to do? How do they see themselves? Each and every question leads to a new discovery about the beautiful shining souls we call "our children."

The key to empowering our children comes with asking them empowering questions. Questions that make them think and feel what is true about themselves. Exploring their likes, their natural interests and talents, all allow them to flourish.

When you ask questions to a very young child, you can see their inner light begin to shine brighter and brighter, realizing that someone is engaged in their world. The questions, the right questions, allow them to share with you their likes and dislikes.

Sometimes it's very hard as an adult not to share our very developed opinions! We are so accustomed to letting others know what we think, we forget that what our small children look for is our approval. They look for our excitement and enthusiasm. Now I am not saying to never give them feedback that is constructive. What I am saying though is to be thoughtful with what we share, how we share it, and when we share it.

Our roles as parents, or as I view my role - guide, is to help them explore themselves and their world in a thoughtful manner, allowing them to truly discover what excites them in life.

Happy, kind, resourceful children should be our goal. When you raise a child with these skills it really doesn't matter what they end up doing for work in life, as long as they are happy and being their best version of themselves they can be. In order to change this world, we need people to bring forward their best versions of themselves. This begins with childhood. Each and every day opportunities arise for us as parents to engage with our children and discover with them what is possible. As you read this book to them, remember the bigger outcome; for us to raise happy, genuinely authentic-to-themselves children. Enjoy each and every moment while you have them.

Thank you,

Kim

if you could imagine just who you would be,
think in your mind, pretend and let's see!

Would you choose to be a farmer who takes care of the fields...

or maybe a brave knight
with a strong mighty shield?

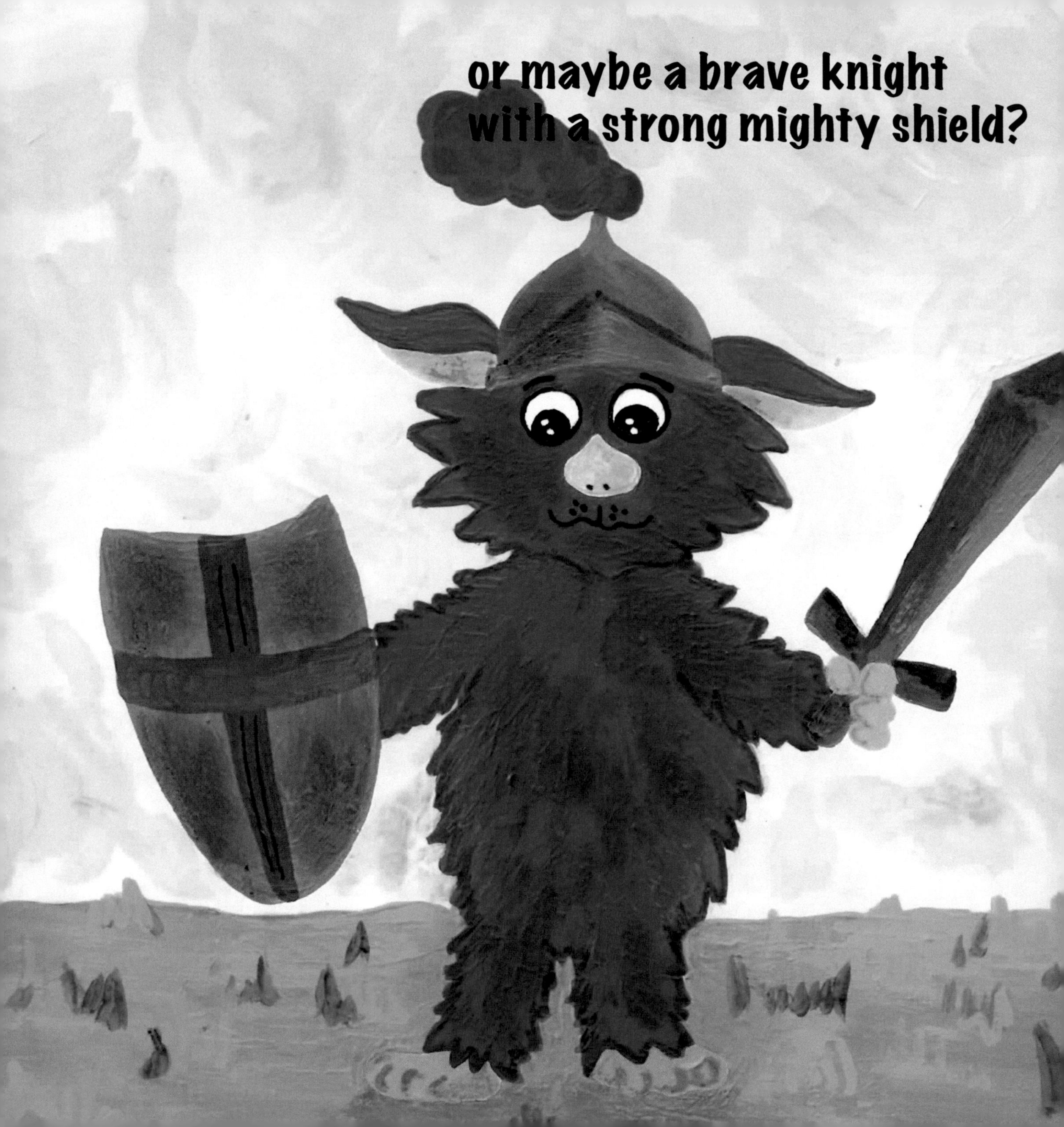

What about a football player
who plays in the big game...

or an artist who paints so beautifully and then signs their name?

there's always a mayor who runs the big city...

or the astronomer who studies the stars
so far off and pretty.

Maybe a scuba diver who swims in the ocean...

or a scientist who brews up a big messy potion.

The engineer who builds the bridge...

the mountaineer with goats
on the ridge.

The photographer who's
pictures show us the world...

The hair dresser who makes sure
your hair stays so curled....

Well here's an idea, maybe something
you'll do, a thought to remember,
whatever life brings to you

it really doesn't matter the work that you pick,
so don't go and make yourself worried or sick.

What matters the most is the
person you are,
your spirit, your love, your
kindness by far...

the way you treat people,
your family and friends,
your toys, your pets, your Self in the end.

This is what counts, the way that you act,
how you choose to be is the true
important fact!

be kind, be loving and oh so happy all of your days
this is the path to follow, the brightest of ways!

So when someone asks you,
"when you grow up what do
you want to be?"

Smile wide and answer...

" **What I do may be work but what i am is me,
the kindest, most loving, best me I choose to be!**

Made in the USA
Middletown, DE
27 January 2021

32474247R00018